Copyright © 1989 by Nord-Süd Verlag, Mönchaltorf, Switzerland. First published
in Switzerland under the title *Lena und der Schneemann*. English translation
copyright © 1989 by Rada Matija AG, North-South Books English language
edition copyright © 1989 by Rada Matija AG, 8625 Gossau ZH, Switzerland.

10 9 8 7 6 5 4 3 2 1

First published in the United States, Great Britain, Canada, Australia
and New Zealand in 1989 by North-South Books, an imprint of Rada Matija AG.

Library of Congress Catalog Card Number: 89-42614.

British Library Cataloguing in Publication Data

Hol, Coby, *1943-*
    Lisa and the snowman.
    I. Title II. Lena und der Schneemann. *English*
    833'.914 [J]

ISBN 1-55858-022-0

LISA AND THE SNOWMAN

Coby Hol

North-South Books
New York

When Lisa woke up one Sunday morning, she heard her friends laughing and shouting outside. She quickly jumped up and went to the window.

"Hurray!" she said. "It snowed last night!"

She quickly got dressed. She put on a warm yellow sweater and the red hat that her grandmother had knitted for her.

When she got outside a snowball fight started.
Everyone was having fun.

In the afternoon Lisa began making a snowman. First, she squeezed together a firm ball
of snow. Next, she put it on the ground and
rolled it until it got bigger and bigger.

Soon, the snowman was almost finished.
Only the buttons for his jacket were missing.
"What a nice snowman!" thought Lisa. "He
almost looks alive."

It was getting dark as Lisa walked home.
She noticed that she had lost her hat.

Her mother said: "Let's see if we can still find your hat." So together they went to look for it.

As they walked through the snow they came to Lisa's snowman. "There's my hat!" yelled Lisa. "Someone must have found it and put it on the snowman's head to keep him warm."

"Lisa needs her hat back," her mother said
to the snowman. "You will be all right in the
cold."

But as Lisa and her mother walked home,
the snowman looked very sad.

As they sat inside by a warm fire, Lisa thought about the snowman. "May I look for a new hat for the snowman in my play-clothes?" she asked.

"Of course you can," said her mother. "I'm sure the snowman would love a new hat."

When Lisa looked through her play-clothes
she found a beautiful clown's hat that she had
worn at a carnival, a Chinese hat that her
mother had made for a school play, and a

battered old hat that her grandfather used to
wear. "The snowman will love one of these,"
she thought.

The next day, Lisa put all the hats into a bag
and went to see the snowman.
   First, she tried on the clown's hat. Lisa
thought it looked very nice, but the snowman
didn't look happy.

Then she tried on the Chinese hat. Lisa thought it looked even better, but the snowman looked very sad.

Finally, Lisa tried the old hat that her grandfather used to wear. She stood back and watched
as the snowman smiled.
  Now everyone was happy.

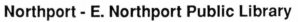